Aw

Written by
Elizabeth Dale

Illustrated by
Iain Carroll

Ransom

I wake suddenly in my bed.

I was having a bad dream.

I sit up and look around, panting.

Everything looks strange.

The house is quiet.

My room is tidy.
There are no books or clothes on the floor.

My room is *always* untidy.

Slowly I go downstairs.

The house is still very quiet.
No one is here.

Did everybody go out and forget
me?

The telephone rings and the answerphone clicks in.

"Hello!" a woman says.
"I'm so sorry ... I'm so very sorry."

Then she cries.

Why is she crying?

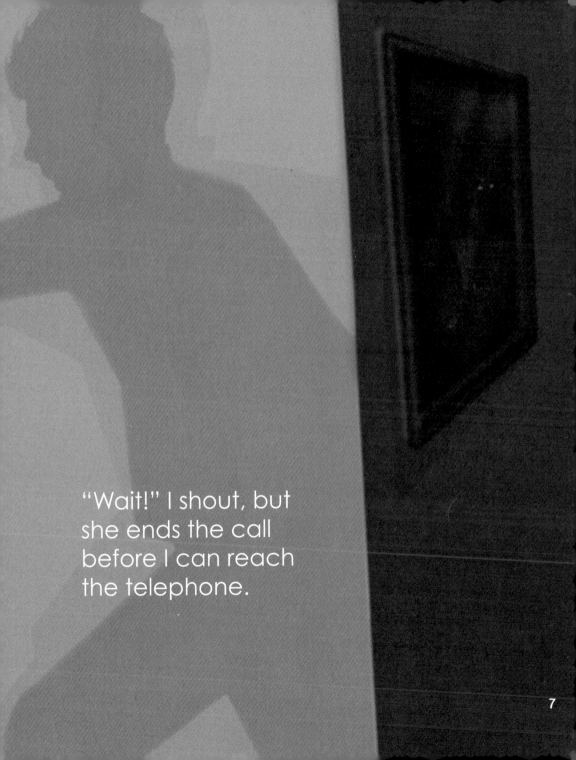

"Wait!" I shout, but she ends the call before I can reach the telephone.

I look around.
The kitchen and living room are tidy.

I have never seen the house looking
so clean.

"Mum!" I call, but my voice echoes.
Everywhere is quiet.

I wander around.

The house feels strange and empty.

I feel empty.

In the kitchen, I open the fridge.

The fridge isn't empty. It's full of food: tarts, pies and snacks.

I smile. We must be having a party.

That's why the house is so clean and tidy!

Then I hear people coming down the path.

They open the front door and step inside.

I see my aunts, uncles and cousins talking quietly. They look sad.

If we are having a party, why are people sad?

I look at the calendar in the kitchen.

For today there is just one word
written on it: 'Chris'.

That's my name.

I smile.
They did not forget me!

I hear a noise and turn around.

My mum walks into the kitchen.

I see tears in her eyes.

I rush to her, but she does not see me.

I try to hug her, but she walks straight through me.

My arms close around nothing.

"Oh Chris," she says to herself.
"I miss you. I'll never forget you."